MISH

RELAXES!

Pete frowned at the bathroom door. The sound of splashing came to him. Quickly he looked toward the open door to his room and back to the bathroom door.

"Mish!" he whispered at the door crack. "Let me in!"

More splashing.

He went around then, through his parents' bedroom, through their dressing room and to the door which opened into the bathroom on that side. Quickly he opened it.

Mish lay in the tub, reclining luxuriously with his four legs up. Mrs. Peter's lavender bath bubbles rose from the surface. . . .

Mishmash

and the
Substitute Teacher

Molly Cone

Illustrated by Leonard Shortall

AN ARCHWAY PAPERBACK
POCKET BOOKS · NEW YORK

POCKET BOOKS, a Simon & Schuster division of
GULF & WESTERN CORPORATION
1230 Avenue of the Americas, New York, N.Y. 10020

Published by arrangement with Houghton Mifflin Company
Library of Congress Catalog Card Number: 63-18441

ISBN: 0-671-29934-4

First Pocket Books printing February, 1979

10 9 8 7 6 5 4 3 2 1

Trademarks registered in the United States and other countries.

Printed in the U.S.A.

TO
GARY

1

"I SEE in the papers that the world is coming to an end," said Mr. Peters, reading the newspaper at the breakfast table. He chuckled.

Pete swallowed his bite of toast. "When?" he said.

His mother looked at his father and frowned, warningly.

"Not this afternoon," she said hastily to Pete.

Mr. Peters shrugged. "It doesn't say this afternoon," he agreed.

Pete munched his crisp cereal thoughtfully. If it wasn't this afternoon it wouldn't do him much good, he thought. For the test would be this afternoon—the test the substitute teacher had prepared for them.

Thinking about the test, Pete plopped into his seat at school with an unnecessary plunk. Miss Dingley frowned at him.

She wasn't anything like the regular teacher. She had a dried-up face and watery blue eyes. Her hands were brown and wrinkled and her dress was wrinkled too. Miss Dingley was the kind who didn't care much how she looked. She was the kind who went out and looked under rocks at the beach and brought things she found to school in old Mason jars. Yesterday she had brought some green stuff which floated in the small aquarium on her desk. Miss Dingley was living in the regular teacher's house while she was gone, and taking care of Miss Patch's dog.

The regular teacher's dog, Mishmash, used to be Pete's dog. Pete sighed a little, remembering how he had answered the advertisement for a puppy on the first day of school that year, and how he had come home with Mishmash.

Mishmash was no puppy; he was a big

4

black friendly dog. He was the friendliest dog Pete's mother and father had ever seen. He was so friendly that the people who lived in Pete's neighborhood locked their front doors to keep Mishmash from walking in.

Nobody had really appreciated a dog like Mishmash, Pete reflected, except his teacher, Miss Patch. She had liked the big dog at once. She had told Pete that Mishmash was the nicest present she had ever received. Even now, Pete's chest swelled at the thought of her pleasure.

Soberly, Pete regarded Miss Dingley. He wished it was Miss Patch with her good loud voice, and her teeth sticking out in a friendly way when she smiled. Miss Dingley's smile looked pasted on. Suddenly Pete felt sorry for Mishmash having to stay with the substitute teacher. He wondered how Mishmash was getting along with Miss Dingley.

His thoughts snapped back to the test. He wished he could find out more about the test. Pete left his seat and went to the front of the room. He pretended he was interested in looking at the aquarium.

"Algae," said Miss Dingley, looking at him sharply.

Pete made quite a show of gazing at the

greenish water as if he could really make out something in it. Miss Dingley watched him.

Figuring out how to ask her about the test, Pete said, "How's Mishmash?"

Her mouth grew small with disapproval. "I have to keep the gate locked," she said sternly.

He must have unlatched it, thought Pete. Mishmash was pretty good at opening and closing things. Pete wondered if Mishmash had insisted on eating Miss Dingley's breakfast instead of his own. He wondered if the dog had pushed her into the closet and

closed the door. Pete grinned at the thought of that!

Miss Dingley looked at him suspiciously. Quickly Pete went to his seat. He guessed Mishmash missed Miss Patch.

Miss Dingley rapped her pencil on the edge of the desk for the class's attention. "Fractions," she announced. "First, we're going to review fractions."

Thinking about Miss Patch, Pete spoke up: "First on Fridays, we always have a current events discussion."

Miss Dingley looked down the long row until her eyes found him. The displeasure was still on her face. Leonard McCurdy snickered. Miss Dingley's glance jumped to him.

Leonard McCurdy was the biggest boy in the room. He was the biggest boy in the whole school. Sometimes Pete practiced saying to himself, "Leonard McCurdy and me," or "Me and Leonard McCurdy." Usually he couldn't help smiling even when he said it only in his mind.

"I will write two fractions on the board," Miss Dingley said as if there had been no interruption. She wrote the two fractions. "Now tell me which is the larger number?"

She pointed with her chalk to Leonard Mc-Curdy.

Pete looked at the numbers on the board. They were 1/4 and 1/16. He turned in his seat to see Leonard McCurdy.

Leonard stood up. "The larger fraction is 1/16," he said confidently.

From her seat in front of Leonard, Wanda Sparling giggled.

Miss Dingley, who had raised the chalk to write another pair of numbers on the board, turned around. She consulted her seating chart and then she looked over Wanda's head at Leonard McCurdy. "Do you mean to tell me that if you were offered your choice of one-fourth of a pie or one-sixteenth of a pie, you would choose the one-sixteenth size?"

Leonard McCurdy glanced around at the sly grins on the faces of his classmates. "Sure!" he said in his big voice. He looked Miss Dingley straight in the eye. "Because I don't like pie!"

The class laughed. A smile came over Miss Dingley's face, a thin stretchy smile, and then it was quickly gone.

She likes him, thought Pete. And he remembered that Miss Patch had always laughed at the things Leonard McCurdy did.

"Our test will be given immediately following recess period this afternoon," Miss Dingley announced.

The grin that Pete had tried on in reflection of Leonard McCurdy's slipped off.

"It will cover everything you have had—or were supposed to have had," she put in. She leaned against the edge of the desk and folded her arms. "Some teachers don't believe in tests," she said.

She meant their regular teacher, thought Pete. A feeling of fondness for his regular teacher came over him.

"But I do!" said Miss Dingley. "I believe in giving tests because life is nothing more than a series of tests." She raised her voice a little so that the boy who jiggled in his seat in the back row would be sure to hear her. "And the sooner you learn to meet life's tests, the better off you'll be."

Pete opened his text and wondered how many chapters the examination would cover.

"You either know your work or you don't!" Miss Dingley said, and Pete snapped the book closed. She was frowning at him.

It seemed to Pete as if she were frowning at him most of the rest of the day. She pursed her lips when he accidentally knocked over

9

the wastepaper basket. She shook her head at him when he went up to sharpen his pencil. She tapped her pencil against the edge of her desk and propelled him reluctantly to his seat when the end-of-recess bell rang.

When it was time to take the test, Pete felt his heart begin to beat faster. It seemed to thump loudly, echoing its beat in his throat. It set up a distant ringing in his ears. Pete closed his eyes and tried quickly to remember what he had learned so far. Nothing came to his mind—nothing at all. Suddenly he felt a little sick.

The boy seated behind nudged him. Pete opened his eyes. He looked to the front of the room. Something strange was happening to the aquarium on the teacher's desk. Something that turned the greenish water into pink bubbles. Enormous pink bubbles which crowded to the top and bounced out. There was a gasp from Miss Dingley.

As if it were a signal, the class burst into laughter. The laughter rose and slapped against the blackboard. Pete couldn't help it. His own laughter was loud, louder than John Williams', louder even than Leonard McCurdy's, louder than anyone else's in the room.

Miss Dingley stood in front of the class, her mouth pressed tight. "Will the person who put the bubbles in the bowl, please step to the front of the room," she said. And then said it again, louder, over the noise.

The laughing stopped. Pete looked around. He wondered who did it. No one moved in the back of the room; no one moved in the front. He looked at Miss Dingley. There was no mistaking it.

She was looking straight at him.

2

THE ROOM was so still that the hands of the clock seemed to jerk violently as the minutes moved on. No one spoke.

Miss Dingley went to her desk and sat down. She sat there waiting, waiting until the class began to shift in their seats and heads craned from one side of the room to the other. But her eyes did not waver.

Miss Dingley's glance lay fixed on him. Pete looked up once and quickly away again. He squinched down in his seat, feeling the red crawl up behind his neck, feeling it cover his face. Silently he studied his fingers. He looked guilty, he knew. For no reason, he even felt guilty.

I didn't do it, Pete said loudly inside himself. But his lips were too stiff to move, and no one heard him.

The bell rang and still they sat. Miss Dingley stood up. "The test will be given on Monday," she said. "Class dismissed."

Pete's shoulders twitched as he walked out of the classroom away from her gaze. Wanda Sparling caught up with him.

"You're lucky," she said. "We don't have to take the test until Monday."

Pete looked at her sharply. Wanda lived next door to him. Too close, if you asked him.

Wanda smiled an innocent smile. "The morning newspapers said the world is coming to an end," she said, and gave a little skip.

Pete scowled. As far as he was concerned it could end any time. Preferably before Monday.

"The seven o'clock news said Sunday afternoon at three o'clock," she said with authority. "In India everybody is praying and apologizing to everybody else and giving all their worldly goods away to be ready for doomsday. I'm going to get busy right now and make an escape shelter!"

Pete looked at her pityingly.

"You can help me," she offered generously.

"Thanks," he said dryly, but his thoughts had jumped back to Miss Dingley and the aquarium.

"If I were you," said Wanda philosophically, "I'd just take off—until Miss Patch comes back."

"You talk as if I was the one who did it!" His voice came out hoarse.

Wanda shrugged. "You didn't tell her you didn't," she said.

Pete watched her as she turned up the walk to her house and disappeared inside. Then he swung around and walked rapidly back the way he had come. He passed the school, crossed the street to the other side, and kept walking.

As he walked he practiced what he would say to Miss Dingley when he saw her. First he would ring the doorbell of her house, he decided, and when she came to the door he would just explain how he didn't do it. It was simple enough, he figured. All he had to do was to explain.

The house Miss Dingley lived in was surrounded by a heavy wire fence. Along the fence on the inside grew a thick laurel hedge. It was impossible to see through the fence because of the hedge. It was impossible to see over the fence, and the only way to get to the house was by the gate. Pete stopped before the gate.

He looked through it to the house. The window shades had been raised at all angles. When Miss Patch lived there the shades had been either all up or all down.

The gate did not move under Pete's hand. It was not just latched, but locked, with a chain and padlock. Pete stared through the gate to the door of the house. It looked as if Miss Dingley had not come home from school yet. He decided to wait.

"Here, Mishmash," he called in a low voice through the gate, while he was waiting. But no big black dog bounced out to greet him. He wondered whether Mishmash could be in the house. He climbed on the gate and tried to see into the windows whose shades were up. No black dog's face could be seen. Mish was not in the house; that was plain to see.

Pete moved down the fence side. "Here, Mish!" he called through the thick hedge. He wondered whether the dog would

recognize his voice, if he heard him. "Hey, Mish," he called softly, pressing his face against the fence wire. "You, there!" He moved slowly around the corner to the back of the house, calling softly every few feet.

Mishmash for a time had been his dog. Pete sighed. His mother hadn't gotten along with Mishmash. Nor his father either. Only Miss Patch, with her teeth which stuck out when she smiled and her hearty laugh, had really appreciated a dog like Mish.

Suddenly Pete heard a snuffling on the other side of the hedge.

"Mish?" he called. "Hey, boy, that you?"

The snuffling increased. In front of Pete, on the other side of the fence, there was a tearing of leaves, and Mish's black head burrowed through the shrubbery.

Pete had to laugh. "Hi, boy," he said.

The dog grinned at him through the hole in the bushes. Then he dropped down and began to dig with great industry at the earth below the fence.

Pete poked his hand through the fence wire and patted Mish's head. "What are you looking for, Mish? A bone? Did you bury a bone?"

But the hole Mish was digging was already

becoming too deep and too wide for a mere bone. Mish stopped digging and poked his nose down into the hole. He burrowed a moment, and then his nose appeared under and on Pete's side of the fence.

"Stop that, Mish!" cried Pete. "You can't do that!" But Mishmash was too busy to listen to Pete. Pete looked over his shoulder at the sound of a car. It was an old blue one. Miss Dingley had a blue car.

Pete dropped to his knees. He pushed Mish's nose back under the fence and began shoveling back dirt with his own hands to fill the hole.

The blue car stopped. It was Miss Dingley's car. Pete stood up quickly, his back to the fence, hoping that Miss Dingley wouldn't notice the hole at his heels.

Miss Dingley's eyes swept over him. She looked at his hands covered with fresh dirt. She looked at the new earth turned up under the fence. As she looked, Mishmash stuck his nose through the hole again and to the outside of the fence. Miss Dingley glanced from the hole to Pete's hands and back to the hole again. Her eyes gleamed accusingly.

Pete gulped. Miss Dingley thought that he had been trying to dig the dog out. She thought he was trying to steal Mishmash!

Pete turned and ran. He ran as fast as he could. He wondered whether Miss Dingley could run fast enough to catch up with him. But he didn't turn around to see.

When he was half a block away, Pete heard a car start up, and for a moment he could hardly breathe. The car honked at him.

"Hi Pete!" shouted Mr. Turkle, waving at Pete from the front seat of his truck. Mr. Turkle lived in the house on the top of the hill.

Weakly Pete waved back, but he didn't stop running. He cut across a cleared lot where a bulldozer was digging a big square hole, and he bent low, moving from one stack of lumber to the next until he had reached the other street. Then he flew past Mrs. Engstrom's house and past Mrs. Barnes'. Next to Wanda's house was an empty lot. Pete jumped wildly over the scraggly underbrush until he reached the center of the lot. There he ducked behind a Scotch broom bush covering the open end of a hole which he knew to be there, and flung himself into it. He landed, gasping for breath, on the dirt floor.

3

"I'VE BEEN expecting you," said Wanda.

She sat in the middle of the cave on an orange crate. An old candy box lay open in her lap. In it was a jumble of bright beads and buttons.

Pete picked himself up.

"I'm deciding which to take—my pink pearl, or my shell bracelet. I am allowing myself to save only one. Every inch of space will count," she told him importantly.

Pete frowned.

"You can bring only your favorite

things," she dictated. "As, for instance, your baseball bat." She stopped to reflect. "Although, I really doubt that there will be much time for games when the world comes to an end."

Pete would have liked to turn around and go out, but the thought of Miss Dingley out there kept him where he was. He stayed, though he had no intention of staying very long.

Wanda giggled. "Won't everybody be mad when the end of the world comes and it'll be too late to do anything?"

"How do you know it'll come?" Pete tried not to think of Miss Dingley thinking he had gone to her house to steal her dog.

"It said so in the newspapers."

"What's this?" he asked, nudging a plastic bag with his toe.

"My best dress," she said. "It's got two petticoats."

Pete kept the smile inside his face as his father often did. "Got any matches?"

She nodded. "And a frying pan. I would have taken my mother's old coffeepot, except it was an electric percolator." She added, "Personally, I don't care much for coffee."

He looked around. "It's pretty small," he pointed out. He examined the walls. They were of hard gray clay, almost as smooth as the cement walls in his basement. For a dugout, it was a neat little room. Suddenly he was interested in spite of himself.

"Why don't we start digging back?" he proposed. "We could dig way back. Maybe we could dig a room big enough for our whole families—maybe even for the whole block!" Miss Dingley lived several blocks away. "Of course," he added with a show of regret, "we couldn't possibly make it big enough for more than one block of families."

Wanda gave him a withering look. "We couldn't possibly make it big enough for everyone on this block," she said. "We can't make it big enough for everyone in both our families—not big enough for everyone in even one of our families. We can make it only big enough for me and you! Although why I should bother my head saving you is more than I know." She rolled her eyes heavenward.

"Don't do me any favors!" retorted Pete. He glanced out, wishing he had never come in.

"Besides, my mother and father aren't much interested. I've been warning them and warning them," Wanda said with a martyred air, "and all they do is laugh. The whole world is coming to an end—and they laugh!" She threw up her hands.

Pete thought of his own parents. His father had thought the whole thing was really funny, too, he remembered. Reluctantly, he said, "I guess you're right."

They set to work clearing the floor of the cave of sticks and stones. Every time Pete carried some rubble to the door of the cave to be dumped outside, he stuck his head out first, peered around the bush, and looked up and down the street, before he stepped out. Once he thought he saw a blue car in the distance, and he stepped back so quickly that he bumped into Wanda who was just behind him.

"Ow!" she shrieked.

He turned quickly and put his hand over her mouth. "Be quiet!" he commanded.

She jerked away from his grasp. "There's no law that says I can't say 'ow' when I want to," she told him fiercely.

He peered out once more, and breathed more easily when he saw that what he had taken for the teacher's car was only a gardener's old blue truck. Boldly he faced Wanda. "When I say 'quiet,' " he directed, "you've got to be quiet."

She glared at him. "Since when?" she challenged.

"Since right now. Someone's got to be boss of this outfit," he declared.

"Well, it was my idea in the first place so I'll be boss," said Wanda.

"It makes no difference whose idea it was," Pete pointed out. "The important thing is what you contribute." He felt pleased with her attention. "The boss should be chosen on the basis of his contributions."

Wanda smiled happily. "In that case, I'm boss. I contributed the frying pan, the candle, the matches, the box of chocolate-covered graham crackers, the bag of popcorn, the—"

He interrupted her with a wave of his hand. "Not that kind of contribution."

Suspiciously she looked at him.

He flexed his arm. "I mean the contribution of muscle—and mind and courage!" It sounded fine. It sounded brave and fine.

"I'm not afraid of anything," said Wanda.

Pete thought of all the things girls were supposed to be afraid of. "Lizards?" he suggested.

Wanda shook her head.

"Green caterpillars? Mice?"

"Pooh!" said Wanda. "Who's afraid of mice!"

"Suppose a bear came toward you? I guess you wouldn't be afraid, would you?"

"When the world comes to an end, there won't be any bears," said Wanda confidently.

"Oh yes there will! Bears live underground all the time. If a cave could save you, it could save bears too. Bears and cougars, maybe—and hungry little wolves!" Pete growled a slow gurgling sound.

Wanda looked only half convinced. She stuck her hands into her pockets, withdrew one hand with a lifesaver stuck to her fingers, picked off the lint, and popped the candy into her mouth. She sucked at it.

Pete looked at her calculatingly. "If I'm boss I'll make my mother give us a big jar of strawberry jam and a gallon of her green pickles."

Wanda swallowed her candy. "I love green pickles!" she said.

Pete looked around, proudly surveying his kingdom. "After breakfast tomorrow, we'll bring some boards over from my basement and make a door. You get out here as soon as you've eaten your breakfast," he commanded.

Wanda made a face at him. "I'll think about it—after I see those pickles!" She went out of the cave and climbed the mound of dirt beside its opening. Standing on the top of the hill she grinned down at him. "I'm very particular about pickles," she said.

"I'm not bringing any old pickles until you make up your mind!" Pete hollered at her from the entrance to the cave.

"Suit yourself!" Wanda called back over her shoulder, and ran home.

Pete shrugged and left the cave without a backward look. He didn't really believe the world was coming to an end anyway.

4

Leonard McCurdy and John Williams crossed the street as Pete left the empty lot.

"You going to confess to Miss Dingley?" John Williams inquired with a sly grin.

Pete shook his head and kept walking. Even the mention of Miss Dingley's name made him feel uncomfortable. The two boys dropped into step beside him.

Leonard McCurdy laid his arm companionably about Pete's shoulders. "Of course he's not," Leonard said. "It was a neat trick. I can tell you I would have been proud to have been the one to think of it myself!''

"Me too!" said John Williams, putting his arm about Pete too.

"I didn't do it," said Pete, but he only mumbled it, for Leonard McCurdy had never sought him out before. He had never spoken as much as two words to him. It made Pete feel good to be walking along next to Leonard McCurdy. It made him feel better than he had felt all day.

"Well, how goes it?" asked his father at the dinner table. "Anything much happen today—like the world coming to an end or something?" He smiled around the table.

Mrs. Peters looked at him with a worried face. "Pilferers," she said. "Somebody helped himself to the bag of groceries I set out on the porch about a half hour ago."

"You mean someone walked off with it?" asked Pete.

Mrs. Peters shook her head. "That's what I can't understand," she said. "Whoever it was merely helped himself to a handful of walnuts and a few oranges." She looked out the window, still frowning. "I really can't understand it."

Mr. Peters shrugged. "Probably the oranges rolled out," he suggested.

"And the nuts," said Mrs. Peters dryly. "No doubt they just jumped out of the bag and cracked themselves all over the sidewalk."

"Perhaps a squirrel," said Mr. Peters, not much concerned. Pete nodded. "Me and Leonard McCurdy," he said, puffing up a little, "batted a ball around after school."

"How's the substitute teacher?" Mrs. Peters asked him.

Pete looked away. "All right, I guess."

"Who's Leonard McCurdy?" his father inquired as his mother went into the kitchen to get something from the oven.

Pete smiled. "Me and Leonard McCurdy are planning to get together tomorrow maybe to ride our bikes around Green Lake." John Williams had planned to go too, but it didn't occur to Pete to mention it.

"Who did you say Leonard McCurdy was?" his mother asked, coming back and setting a pot of coffee on the table.

"Just one of the guys in my room at school." Pete shrugged, Leonard McCurdy's shrug.

"Wanda Sparling was here a moment ago inquiring for you," Mrs. Peters remarked.

"You don't say!" Pete said in Leonard McCurdy's voice.

His mother frowned. "She said to tell you she expects you to help her finish building something or other."

Pete snorted. Unfortunately the snort occurred right in the middle of a gulp of milk and the milk splashed up and blobbed over his nose. Quickly he set the glass down.

His father regarded him matter-of-factly. "You and Leonard McCurdy had better go wash your face," he said.

Pete pushed his chair from the table and went upstairs to the bathroom. The door to his bedroom was ajar and he glanced in. An orange peel lay on his braided rug. Pete stopped. He hadn't eaten any oranges in his room that day.

He pushed open the door and went in. He looked at the peel on the rug a little while, then he dropped quickly to his knees and looked under the bed. More orange peels. Pete got up and scratched his head. He walked slowly toward the closet, put his hand on the closet door and held it there, listening. He thought he heard a slight sound.

Quickly he pulled open the door. His clothes were in a jumble on the floor. A big black jumble. The jumble moved. A bright black eye peered at him from under the folds

of cloth. The mound moved and a big black head raised itself and grinned at him.

"Mishmash!" cried Pete.

Mishmash rose and shook himself. He stepped over the muddle of shoes and jackets and jumped to the middle of the bed. He stretched; he yawned, a big noisy yawn. Pete laughed. Then quickly, he went to the bedroom door and closed it.

Mishmash grinned back at him. The dog settled himself with his chin on his paws, rolled his eyes at Pete, and closed them.

"You ran away!" Pete said.

Mish opened his eyes and closed them again.

Pete sat down on the edge of the bed, his head in his hands. How was he going to explain to Miss Dingley, he wondered. And then the full trouble struck him. Miss Dingley would not only think Pete had tried to steal Mishmash but now she would have proof that he did! Pete groaned. He thought fast. There was only one thing to do that he could see.

"I've got to keep you here, Mish," he said. "I've got to hide you here until Miss Patch comes home!"

Quickly he looked around the room. It

was all right for the night. But where could he keep Mishmash during the day?

Pete thought of his father and how he always backed up Pete's mother. Pete frowned. Then he thought of Wanda's cave. The shelter would be a good hideout for Mishmash. Thinking about it, Pete smiled. He put his arms around the dog.

"If the world should come to an end, it'll be you and me together," he whispered. As an afterthought, he added—"and Wanda."

5

"IT LOOKS like a bush," said Pete with satisfaction, standing off to view the entrance to the cave. He had put together a door out of pieces of old lumber, and over the door he had fastened a big bunch of Scotch broom.

"Camouflage," said Wanda approvingly.

"When we pull that little old door over the front of the shelter, no one would ever know there was a cave there. Not even if they walked right past it," Pete pointed out.

Wanda looked at him reflectively.

"Besides, we have Mishmash to guard for us."

Wanda snorted. "Fine guard Mishmash will be," she said. "He doesn't even know the meaning of the word."

"Sure he does," said Pete. "Here, Mish!" he called, pointing to the doorway of the cave. "On guard!"

Mishmash came instantly. He scrambled down the hill, leaped at Pete and licked his face fondly with his wet tongue.

"No!" said Pete. "Quit it now, Mish, y'hear me? Cut it out! I said 'Guard'!" He pushed the dog away. "Get it? Guard!"

Mishmash lay down. He rolled over, stuck his four feet into the air and closed one eye. The other gleamed at Pete.

Wanda laughed. "He's playing dead. He's a crazy mixed-up dog, that's what he is." She added, "Boy! Is your mother going to be mad when she discovers Mishmash is back."

"He's just visiting," said Pete with dignity.

Wanda said, "Personally, my mother doesn't care about having drop-in visitors."

"My mother won't mind," said Pete elaborately.

"Well, it'll just be for one more night anyway," Wanda said significantly.

"He can help us bring in things, can't you, Mish?" said Pete patting the dog.

Mishmash grinned at him with his big tongue hanging out and his eyes shining.

"Much help he'll be," sniffed Wanda. She picked up a carton and dumped its contents on the floor of the cave.

"What do we need an old hot-water bottle for?" asked Pete, picking it up.

"For hot water, silly," said Wanda.

Pete looked at it and then at Wanda. "It's got a hole in it," he said.

"Of course it has," said Wanda busy with the other things from the box. "If it didn't, my mother wouldn't have let me take it."

Pete tossed it back into the box and picked up another item.

"That's a potato masher," Wanda said.

"What do we need a potato masher for!" said Pete, and after a glance at Wanda chimed in with her answer:

"To mash potatoes, silly!"

Wanda glared at him.

Pete stood there with his hands in his pockets looking around. "Seems to me you have too much stuff already."

"We'll need it," she said ominously, and went out and brought in another carton.

Pete looked at its contents with surprise. "What did you bring these old cans of paint for?"

Wanda looked pleased with herself. "It's what's left over from our bathroom," she said. "I thought I'd paint the clay walls pink. They are so nice and smooth they should take paint nicely. I just love pink," she said happily.

He stared at her. "You mean you're going to paint the cave *pink?*"

"Not if you'd really prefer apple green," she said with a generous smile. "I brought the green along too, just in case. *That's* left over from the downstairs bathroom. Personally I prefer pink. It's my opinion that it'll look perfectly lovely in here painted pink!"

He looked around. "Whoever heard of painting a cave pink!"

She shrugged. "Okay, green then."

"Not green!" he couldn't help hollering the words at her. "Not pink either! Not anything! Who cares how it looks!" he shouted, waving his arms around. "If the world really comes to an end, who's going to care about things like that!"

Wanda regarded him unblinking. "Girls care about things like that," she told him.

Pete looked at her in wonder. He let his hands fall to his sides. It had never occurred to him how lucky he was not to be a girl.

Wanda crossed her arms and said huffily, "I don't see the dill pickles. I thought you were going to contribute pickles along with your courage and bravery."

Pete frowned at the sarcasm in her voice.

Mishmash came in carrying something. He set it down at Pete's feet and sat back pleased with himself. Wanda picked it up.

"What's this?" Wanda demanded.

Pete glanced at it briefly. It was a boot, a woman's fur-lined galosh. Pete patted Mish's head. "You just wanted to help too, didn't you, old boy?"

Wanda sniffed. Mishmash darted out and brought back something else which he laid at her feet. It was an old fur piece. "What are we supposed to do with this!" she said taking it and waving it in front of Pete's face.

Pete took it. It looked a little moth-eaten. Mish must have brought that too," he said. "He saw me bring in things and I guess he wanted to help too." Pete couldn't help but show his pride.

Mish bounded out and backed in again, dragging something.

Wanda held up a door mat on which was printed WELCOME.

"Good old Mish," Pete said fondly.

"Good old Mish, m'eye!" sputtered Wanda. "We're not welcoming anybody more around here." She threw it out the door of the cave.

Mish got up, went out, sniffed at it, and obligingly brought it right back.

"Come on, Mishmash," said Pete hastily. "It's almost dinnertime." And stealthily, with the dog at his heels, he made his way home.

6

PETE looked through the window of his back door into the kitchen. Not seeing anyone, he opened the door, twisting the knob slowly so there would be no sound.

"Come on, Mishmash," he whispered, and taking hold of the dog's collar he moved silently across the kitchen, through the entry way and up the stairs. Quietly he went down the hall to his bedroom.

He closed the bedroom door firmly behind Mishmash and carefully retraced his steps. Outside again, he turned, opened the door noisily, and slammed it behind him.

"I'm home!" he yelled.

His mother came in from the other room. "There's no doubt about *that,*" she remarked, and looked at him closely. She sniffed in delicate little sniffs. "Whew!" she said. "All you'd have to do is bark, and I'd call you Rover."

Pete looked at her uneasily.

She smiled at him. "Why don't you take a good warm bath before you change for dinner."

Pete looked down at his clothes. It hadn't occurred to him to change for dinner.

"I think it would be a good idea," Mrs. Peters said gently.

Pete went on upstairs and into the bathroom. He started the water running in the tub and went into his own room.

"Move over," he nudged Mishmash, as he sat on the bed.

Mish rose on his forelegs and regarded him. "You have to be quiet, Mish," Pete advised him. "Mom doesn't know you're here—and I don't want her to. Understand?"

Mish grinned at him. He jumped off the bed and belly-crawled to the half-opened door, stuck his nose out, withdrew it and came back the same way.

Pete laughed. "You've got the idea," he said.

He went to the closet then to look for his slippers. He knelt on the floor and groped around for a while. Finally he found them, beside his catcher's mitt.

Taking his bathrobe he went on down the hall to the bathroom, whistling loudly.

The bathroom door was closed. The sound of running water came to him. He turned the knob. The door was locked.

"Mom?" he called, "I'm ready to take my bath now!"

She answered from the kitchen: "Take your time!"

Pete frowned at the bathroom door. The sound of splashing came to him. Quickly he looked toward the open door to his room and back to the bathroom door.

"Mish!" he whispered at the door crack. "Let me in!"

More splashing.

He went around then, through his parents' bedroom, through their dressing room and to the door which opened into the bathroom on that side. Quickly he opened it.

Mish lay in the tub, reclining luxuriously with his four legs up. Mrs. Peters' lavender

58

bath bubbles rose from the surface. Pete turned off the water.

"You'd better get out of there!" Pete hissed.

Mishmash leaped out of the tub and rolled over on the bathmat. Pete turned the water-flow handle, and watched as the muddy pink water drained out.

His mother's voice came to him from the hall side. "Through already?" she called to him.

Pete made sure both doors were locked. "Not exactly," he called back. "I'm pretty dirty. Figured I'd better take two baths!"

There was a pause in the steps outside the door. "You're not using any of my good bath salts, are you?"

"Not me!" he said, making a grab for the bath-powder mitt into which Mishmash had just put a paw.

He stood there, listening, until his mother's footsteps had faded away. Then he wrapped Mishmash in a big towel, rubbed him dry and set about to cleaning the tub, refilling it and bathing himself.

"The TV man finally got here today," remarked Mrs. Peters at the dinner table.

"Oh boy!" said Pete.

"The reason it's been so erratic, he said,"

Mrs. Peters explained, "is that the aerial was down—or something like that."

Mr. Peters looked at Mrs. Peters while stirring his coffee. "A lucid man," he remarked dryly.

"He was very nice," said Mrs. Peters. "He assured me that anyone else would have charged us twice as much." She caught the expression on her husband's face. "Not that I really believed him," she put in hastily. "But he was nice."

"Does it work all right now?" asked Mr. Peters.

"I think so." Mrs. Peters poured herself another cup of coffee. "To tell you the truth," she said, "I forgot to test it. He was telling me some interesting things about India. He has a brother who's a government official there." She looked thoughtful. "At least I think he said official."

"Or something like that," put in Mr. Peters.

"The interesting part," Mrs. Peters continued, "was his report about what's happening there. This doomsday thing, you know. Those poor people actually believe it! They actually believe the world is coming to an end! Can you imagine!"

Pete put down his glass of milk.

Mrs. Peters went on. "The schools are all closed, and nobody is going down to business. The prime minister pooh-poohs it, of course. But that doesn't seem to make any difference. The astrologers have predicted the day and the hour—and no one listens to the prime minister anyway."

Pete finished drinking his milk.

Suddenly a startled expression came over his mother's face. Mr. Peters' head jerked up. A loud voice came from the other side of the house, blurred, rose again, and subsided to a mumble.

"It's the TV," said Pete, uneasily.

"What in heaven's name would cause the TV to turn on by itself?" asked his mother rising out of her chair.

"You don't suppose," inquired Pete's father with an innocent air, "that the TV fellow who charged us only half as much figured he might as well come back and make up the other half?"

"Why, that's monstrous!" said Mrs. Peters.

"It's merely a little thought," said Mr. Peters modestly.

The three of them entered the small room off the entryway which served as a den and television viewing room.

"It's off now," said Mr. Peters, flipping the switch on and off again.

Pete looked sharply around the room. A black eye gleamed from behind the corner of the big upholstered rocker.

"Well honestly!" said Mrs. Peters following her husband back into the dining room. "And he seemed so nice, too."

Pete waited until they were gone.

"Mishmash!" he scolded. "You could have waited until I came to turn it on for you, couldn't you? You've got to remember to lay low. Now lay low! Hear me?"

Mishmash rested his jaw on his paw and looked up at Pete. But only for a moment. Then he took a ringside seat before the television set.

"WELL, ladies—" said Mr. Peters, putting his newspaper down, and standing up to welcome the guest who had come by way of the back door. He bowed to Mrs. Barnes in greeting.

"There's a prowler in the neighborhood!" Mrs. Peters announced. Mrs. Barnes nodded.

Hastily Pete closed the TV room door securely behind him.

Mr. Peters opened his eyes wide. "What kind of a prowler?" he asked.

Mrs. Barnes held her fingers up and counted off as she talked. "First," she said, "he made off with Mrs. Engstrom's front-door mat—a brand-new one! Second, he swiped the bottom half of a pair of red and white striped pajamas hanging on Mrs. Chapley's line—"

"Pajamas!" cried Pete in surprise. He didn't remember seeing any red pajamas.

His father looked at him.

Quickly Pete mumbled, "Seems sort of funny to steal pajamas."

"Then!" said Mrs. Barnes, "He took one of *my* new galoshes—with fur lining—" she said in an aside to Mrs. Peters.

"Only one?" murmured Mr. Peters.

Mrs. Barnes nodded. "And—" she went on, "he completely made off with Mrs. Anderson's old fur neckpiece which was hanging over the porch railing to air!"

Mr. Peters pursed his lips and closed his eyes. He seemed to be thinking.

"Sounds to me like your prowler is a one-legged man with a cold." He opened his eyes and looked severely at Pete. "You didn't happen to see a one-legged fellow wearing the bottom half of Mrs. Chapley's pajamas, and Mrs. Anderson's fur piece around his neck, did you?"

"NO SIR!" said Pete grinning with his father.

But the ladies didn't think it was funny at all. Mrs. Barnes said goodbye a little stiffly. Mrs. Peters accompanied her out the front door to the porch.

"Well, I can tell you—" Pete heard Mrs. Barnes say—"if there is any more sneaky pilfering around here, I'm going straight to the police!"

Pete searched his father's face. Had he guessed?

His father said in a low voice, "I don't want to alarm your mother but it does seem rather strange, doesn't it?"

Pete didn't say anything. His mother came in and closed the door and went into the kitchen. She was frowning.

Mr. Peters went back to his newspaper, and Pete put his hand on the knob of the TV room door. The doorbell rang. Slowly Pete turned, and went to answer it.

Mr. Turkle stood outside. "D'you mind if I borrow your telephone?" he asked politely.

Mrs. Peters sang out from the kitchen, "Come right in, Mr. Turkle!" Mr. Peters called, "Help yourself!"

Mr. Turkle sat down at the telephone desk

in the kitchen. He turned the pages of the telephone book slowly. "Some kid must have loosened the brake on my truck—" he explained as he looked up the number.

"Oh my!" said Mrs. Peters.

Pete made himself small behind the door.

"Anyway, it rolled down the hill and hit a fire hydrant. Smashed the whole fender!" Mr. Turkle ran his finger down the column of numbers in the telephone book. "I'm trying to get hold of a garage."

Pete gulped. He remembered something. He remembered that Mishmash loved to ride in cars. He remembered how Mishmash had once jumped into a neighbor's small car and taken over the driver's seat and prevented the woman from keeping her appointment with the dentist. Mr. Turkle lived two blocks away. Uneasily Pete thought of Mishmash sneaking around pilfering things. He could have hopped into that car and—

"Is there something wrong with your telephone line too?" Mrs. Peters asked curiously.

Mr. Turkle finished dialing his number and looked at them as the operator was ringing. "Out of order," he said. "Some fool must have dug a hole, and dug clean into a telephone cable! I'm surprised your service

isn't cut off too. There's not a telephone working in the neighborhood between my house and this one! Hello?'' he said into the telephone. "Is that the Okay Garage?''

Pete backed slowly out of the kitchen—and bumped into Mrs. Barnes who had just opened the front door and come in. Several strands of her hair were hanging over her forehead and her eyes were bulging.

The people in the kitchen turned to her in surprise. "He's gone and done it again!'' said Mrs. Barnes, all out of breath.

"Who?'' said Mr. Turkle, hanging up the telephone.

"What?'' said Mr. and Mrs. Peters together.

Pete stood and listened.

"Someone's gone and stolen my wedding ring! I left it where I always do when I wash dishes—right on the windowsill, next to the plant box. It's gone!''

"Oh, you must be mistaken,'' said Mrs. Peters. "Perhaps you put it somewhere else.''

"It was there,'' Mrs. Barnes said significantly, "when I washed the dishes. It was there—'' she said again, "when I ran over here a few moments ago—and when I went back—it was not there!''

Mr. Peters buttoned his sweater. "Come on, Mrs. Barnes, let's go over and look again. It might be you didn't see it." Mr. Peters took Mrs. Barnes' arm and escorted her out the front door.

Mrs. Peters turned up the heat under the coffeepot. Hastily Pete went into the TV room and closed the door securely behind himself.

Mishmash, his eyes fastened on the television screen, sat unblinking before it. Pete switched off the television set. Mish turned to regard him.

"You can't do things like that!" Pete said to him.

Mishmash closed his eyes and scratched.

Helplessly Pete looked at him. It wasn't safe to let Mishmash run around the neighborhood. It wasn't safe for the neighborhood, he reflected.

Pete waited until he heard Mr. Turkle leave and his mother go back into the kitchen before he led Mishmash up to his bedroom. Dutifully, then, without being told, he put on his pajamas, made his way to the kitchen and munched thoughtfully through a snack of dry cereal and milk.

"It's gone all right!" said Mr. Peters coming in and closing the kitchen door behind him. He locked it carefully. "I advised her to check with the police."

"G'night," said Pete, and quickly went upstairs. He almost ran down the hall to his bedroom, and he opened the door only a crack, squeezed himself in and shut it quickly again. But he needn't have taken such care, for Mishmash was sound asleep in the middle of Pete's bed. Pete stood and looked at him a moment. The dog stirred contentedly in his sleep. Pete gently straightened the dog's ears on the pillow. He pulled the top blanket off the bed and lay down on the rug on the floor. Pete closed his eyes.

A moment later he opened his eyes again and twisted about on the unyielding floor to a more comfortable position. He sat up. The only pillow was squarely under Mishmash's head. Pete pulled the sweater off the chair and placed it on the floor under his head. It was too flat. He reached out, picked up his textbook, wrapped the sweater around it and placed the bundle where his head would lie. Wearily he closed his eyes.

A siren cut through the stillness of the neighborhood. With his eyes shut tight, Pete could see a lineup of police cars led by Miss Dingley's small blue one, crawling up the street. He could see Mrs. Barnes in the front seat of the first car directing the policeman. He could even see Mr. Turkle following the police cars in his truck with the smashed fender. And he could almost hear Mrs. Anderson and Mrs. Engstrom and Mrs. Chapley shouting and pointing as they jumped up and down on their front porches.

Pete rolled over and jumped up. His heart was pounding as he stood over the sleeping dog. He stood there, listening, until the sound of the siren had faded away. Then he drew the covers up over Mish's ears, closed the window, propped a chair up against the door and lay down again.

He wondered whether Mishmash could have swallowed the diamond ring.

8

"Do YOU think they'll put him in jail?" Wanda asked. They sat on the floor of the cave, Sunday morning, Mishmash between them.

Pete snorted. "They can't put dogs in jail."

"They can put dog's *owners* in jail, though," Wanda suggested.

Pete stood up. "You mean Miss Patch? You mean they'll put Miss Patch in jail instead of Mishmash?"

Wanda shrugged. "The owner of a dog in

this city has to be responsible for him, that's what my father said. IF they don't find Mishmash, and IF they can prove he took all the stuff, THEN they'll probably nab Miss Patch just as she comes off the airplane." She added thoughtfully: "They'll get you on count number two for *stealing* the dog."

"Glory!" Pete sat down again.

"Of course, that isn't going to happen," said Wanda with a knowing air.

Pete looked at her.

"The world's coming to an end at three o'clock *today,* remember?" Wanda poked him.

Pete moved away from her jabbing finger. He pulled Mishmash to him and patted the dog. "Most dogs dig up little weensy-teensy bones; Mishmash digs up a colossal telephone cable!"

Wanda snorted. "What makes you think it was Mishmash who dug up the cable? Personally, I think it was more likely the bulldozer clearing that lot over by Mrs. Chapley's. My father said the telephone company will probably sue the construction people."

Pete looked at her reflectively. "I guess you think he didn't swallow the diamond ring either."

Wanda grinned. "Sure he could have swallowed the diamond. Once I swallowed a dime. That little piece of silver is probably sitting inside me, right now." She patted her stomach proudly.

"A little thin dime!" Pete scoffed. "It isn't anywhere near to what a real diamond ring is worth!" For a moment he looked proudly at Mishmash.

"They'll probably make Miss Patch pay what the ring's worth," Wanda said.

Unaccountably Pete felt his Adam's apple bob up and down.

"Anyway, you might as well be hung for a sheep as a goat," said Wanda philosophically.

Pete put his hand up to his collar.

"It's only a figure of speech," she said consolingly.

Pete frowned thoughtfully out the door of the cave. "Just the same," he said finally, "we'd better return those things Mishmash stole. We can return most of them anyway."

Wanda looked at him as if he had gone crazy.

"As soon as Sunday school is over," he directed, "we'll take the stuff back."

She looked down her nose at him. "I'll be busy enough taking things in," Wanda said.

"I'm not going to waste my time taking things out."

"You said yourself we could do without the welcome mat," Pete reminded her.

"I'm beginning to think we could do without a certain d-o-g, too."

He glared at her.

After Sunday school was over, Pete dragged all the stolen stuff out of the shelter, dumped it into a carton and left it on Mrs. Barnes' doorstep with the welcome mat on top. Then he hurried home.

Pete walked through the kitchen. He smelled the chicken roasting in the oven, and looked longingly at the cake with chocolate frosting which glistened on the counter.

"When are we going to eat?" he asked.

His mother glanced at the kitchen clock. And Pete looked too. It was one-thirty. He set his own wristwatch by it.

His mother opened the door of the oven and poked at the chicken. "Not until four, I imagine," she said.

"Not until four!" Pete almost shouted. The world was coming to an end at three and his mother was planning to serve dinner at four!

"You can have a carrot stick," said his mother.

Pete groaned.

Mrs. Peters looked at him curiously. "You had three waffles for breakfast, and a baked apple, if I remember. You can't possibly be hungry already."

Mr. Peters came in and merrily slapped Pete on the head with a folded newspaper.

"What's for dinner?" he asked sniffing at the oven door.

Mrs. Peters laughed. "You, too? Well, perhaps we can scoot dinner ahead to three-thirty, but not a minute earlier."

Pete frowned. "Never mind," he mumbled.

"Isn't it lucky Mrs. Barnes found her diamond ring?" said Mrs. Peters in a happy voice.

"You mean she found it!" Pete's voice was unnecessarily loud in the quiet kitchen.

His father looked at him curiously.

"In the sugar drawer," his mother supplied. "Although how it got from the windowsill to the sugar drawer is a mystery to me!"

Pete breathed a sigh of relief and turned away.

"Say, son," Mr. Peters said as he idly

helped himself to a bunch of grapes from the bowl on the counter. "How did the test go?"

"What test?" said Pete. He glanced at his watch again. He'd have just about enough time to meet Wanda behind the garage and help her take one more load of stuff into the cave. Last-minute stuff, like a toothbrush, and some clothes and maybe even a bar of soap. He opened the back door.

"Just a minute!" said his father.

Slowly Pete shut the door. He turned.

His mother said, looking at him a little oddly, he thought, "Didn't you have a test on Friday?"

Pete took a deep breath. "We were supposed to have the test Friday," he explained, and looked anxiously at them.

Looking interested, they both waited.

"But it was postponed until Monday morning."

"Tomorrow morning?" asked his mother, somewhat unnecessarily, he thought.

Pete nodded.

"You mean you're going to have a test tomorrow morning and you haven't even cracked a book all weekend!" His father put the grapes back into the bowl.

Pete wriggled. "I figured I'd do it—later," he said.

His father said, "I figure you'll do it—right now."

"Right now?" Pete threw a quick glance at the kitchen clock. "It's important that I meet Wanda right now!"

"It's more important that you get to studying right now," said his father.

Pete glanced uncertainly up the stairway in the direction of his room.

"I'll call you when dinner's ready," said his mother brightly.

Pete thought of Wanda waiting for him behind the garage. He thought of Mishmash already in the shelter. He thought of the world coming to an end . . . maybe . . . in less than an hour.

Desperately he said, "I've just got to see Wanda about something!"

His mother turned around to look at him with surprise.

His father silently raised his arm and pointed with a long straight finger up the stairway.

Slowly Pete climbed the stairs.

9

PETE sat down at his desk and opened his book. He turned the pages slowly not seeing anything before him. Downstairs someone knocked loudly on the front door, and he jumped up so fast at the sound that his book fell to the floor.

Pete opened the door to his bedroom and listened. He heard a loud clear voice say, "Can Pete come out to play?" and he breathed a sigh of relief. It was Leonard Mc-Curdy.

"He has some studying to do," Pete heard his father say shortly. "You boys come back later." The door closed and Pete went back to his desk.

He picked up his book from the floor. Something rattled against his window. Curiously he went to it and looked out. Leonard McCurdy and John Williams were standing down below. Seeing him they made motions with their arms. Pete opened the window and leaned out.

"Come on down!" called Leonard McCurdy. John Williams grinned up at him.

"I can't," Pete said, regretfully. "I have to study for the test tomorrow."

"That's just it," said John in a loud whisper. "We've got it figured out so maybe there won't be any test."

"How do you mean?" said Pete.

John nudged Leonard. "You can tell him," he said.

Leonard's grin stretched across his face. "We're going to stick some instant glue on the edges of Miss Dingley's desk drawer!"

John smiled broadly. "That's where she put the test questions. In her top drawer!"

"She won't be able to get the drawer open to get them," said Leonard.

"Boy will she be mad!" said John. "It'll be even better than putting the bubbly stuff in the aquarium!" He turned about and slapped Leonard on the back heartily. "Boy, was that a good trick!"

"You mean Leonard put the stuff in the aquarium!" Pete's voice had risen almost to a shout.

Leonard nodded modestly. "He sure did," said John in admiration.

Mr. Peters' voice could be heard from downstairs. It came up the stairway loudly, into Pete's room, and out the window to the boys below. "Pete!" his father shouted. "I thought I told you to get to your studying!"

At the sound of Mr. Peters' voice, the boys ran. Pete slammed down the window. He stood there thinking about Leonard Mc-Curdy putting the bubbles into the aquarium. He remembered how Miss Dingley's eyes had accused him; how all the class had sat there looking at him as if he had done it. He remembered how he felt when no one got up and admitted to it. How he had wished the world would come to an end right then at that minute.

Pete glanced quickly at his watch. It was twenty minutes to three. Without wasting another moment, he opened his bedroom door, stood listening a moment, and crept silently down the stairs and out the front door.

Wanda met him behind the garage. "We have to work fast," she hissed. "Time's getting short."

"Leonard McCurdy," he said, his voice quivering. "It was Leonard McCurdy all the time!"

Wanda said calmly, "He's a stinker. Everybody knew that."

Pete felt his mouth drop open. "You mean everybody knew it was Leonard McCurdy who fixed the aquarium?"

Wanda's eyes passed over him briefly. "No wonder you're scared of tests," she said. "You can't even put two and two together."

Pete felt his ears getting red. "Come on!" he said. "We haven't got all day."

"I checked everything before Sunday school," said Wanda importantly. "I went over all the supplies. There's two of everything. Two plates, two cups, two bags of peanuts—to tell the truth," she put in, "with all the boxes and things in there, there's just barely enough room for the two of us!"

"Don't forget Mishmash," said Pete quickly.

"He can sit on our laps," said Wanda. "That is—until it's over."

Pete looked at her. Wanda was dressed for the hour in her sister's old Girl Scout uniform. A belt was tied around her middle with things hanging from it: a whistle, a pocket knife, a mirror, a small frying pan.

"I'm supposed to be in my room practicing the trumpet," she said.

Uncomfortably Pete remembered he was supposed to be in his room studying. "They act as if the world's going to last forever," Pete grumbled. "Dinner won't even be ready until three-thirty."

"You mean—won't ever be ready!" said Wanda darkly.

Although he hadn't really believed the world was coming to an end, suddenly there was an odd feeling in Pete's stomach. He thought of his mother and father sitting placidly in their house . . .

"Well—come on!" said Wanda looking back at him.

Slowly he followed her around the house. They made their way, single file, stealthily, to the door of the shelter. Pete turned around once more—one look back. Silently (just in case it might happen) he said good-bye to the house and the people in it. He pushed at the door to the cave.

"No trespassing!" said a loud clear voice.

Wanda screeched and Pete blinked. Leonard McCurdy was sitting on the floor of the cave, sitting and grinning at them. Leonard McCurdy and John Williams.

10

"You GET out of there this instant!" shouted Wanda.

"We like it here," said John Williams. "Don't we, Leonard?" He nudged Leonard McCurdy. "We like it here extremely well."

Leonard McCurdy leisurely put his hands behind his head. "Sure was nice of you to go to all this trouble—for us," he added.

Pete looked at his watch. It said a quarter to three. Fifteen minutes. He licked his lips. He looked at Leonard sitting there grinning. He thought of Leonard, sitting grinning as the teacher's eyes accused the wrong one. Pete made a flying leap.

"Oomph!" said Leonard McCurdy as Pete's knee hit him in the stomach.

John turned his head to watch, and Wanda jumped on him. It was over in a moment. Leonard sat on top of Pete and grinned triumphantly, and with one push John had shoved Wanda and all her Girl Scout equipment out the cave entrance.

Furiously Wanda threw herself back in, and was just as unceremoniously hurled out again.

"You can come back in," Leonard called, "if you promise to be a good girl and sit still."

"I have no intention of sitting still," hollered Wanda. "I'd rather die than sit still!"

Leonard shrugged. "Suit yourself," he said.

Lying on his back with Leonard holding his arms down, Pete twisted.

"It's five minutes to three!" reported John Williams.

With a heave, Pete thrust Leonard over and made a dash out of the cave. He stood on the hilltop, next to Wanda, and they watched silently as the big door was slowly laid into place.

There was a scurrying behind them and turning they perceived Mishmash hurrying toward them with the welcome mat dragging under his feet. As Pete watched him, his eyes blurred.

"Come here, Mish," said Pete, but the words choked in his mouth.

"Well, ta-ta," said Leonard with his face in the crack. The door was finally secured. There was silence.

"You didn't have to sacrifice yourself for *me!*" said Wanda looking at him sideways.

Pete hadn't been thinking of Wanda. "Forget it," he said.

"I'll never forget it!" she said. "Never as long as I live!" She listened to what she had said and giggled.

Mishmash moved in between them, standing with his hind feet on the welcome mat, his front legs resting on their shoulders. Pete swallowed hard. They looked out from the top of the hill up to the sky.

The world was about to come to an end—any minute now, maybe. He wondered if the world would end with a flash of fire. He wondered if the earth would open and swallow them up. Without conscious thought, he tensed himself for a flash or roar.

"It's almost three," Wanda whispered.

Suddenly Pete could not even lift his arm to look at his watch. He felt his eyes drawn to the face of the church steeple clock. Its big hand rested only seconds away from the hour. Pete closed his eyes. "Ten," he counted, waiting for the end of the world. "Ten, nine, eight, seven, six, five, four, three, two—"

There was a loud clatter. A screen door banged and a wind whirled the dust up around them. They heard the sound of a voice.

"Wanda Sparling!" her mother shouted at them. "If I've told you once, I've told you a hundred times—get in here and do your practicing! Do you hear me?"

Pete opened his eyes. He looked at Wanda. Together they looked at the face of the steeple clock. It was one minute past three. They waited until the hand jerked to two minutes after three. Mishmash dropped down and wrestled with the welcome mat.

The world hadn't come to an end. Pete suddenly knew it wasn't going to come to an end after all. Wanda snickered.

"I guess I'd better go in and do my practicing," she said.

Pete let his breath out slowly. "Guess I might as well go in too," he said offhandedly. "I have some studying to do."

"Here Mish," he called halfheartedly.

But Mishmash was busy. He had dragged the welcome mat to the top of the mound just over the entrance to the cave. Here he was busy throwing dirt and gravel over it as if he meant to bury it.

"Come on, Mish," said Pete.

The door to the cave was pushed away. The heads of Leonard McCurdy and John Williams cautiously poked out. Mishmash stopped digging and looked curiously down upon their heads. Then with his big mouth open in a grin, with his tongue hanging out, and his tail wagging, he pushed the welcome mat, dirt, rocks, gravel and all over the edge.

"Hey!" shouted Leonard and John, throwing their arms out and bumping into each other. The dirt rained down on their heads.

"Pfooey!" spat John who had looked up with his mouth open.

The welcome mat hit Leonard McCurdy smack on his back. "Cut that out!" he hollered.

Mishmash answered—with a joyous bark, and dutifully ran after Pete.

Pete walked toward the house. There was still tomorrow, he thought suddenly—and Mishmash, and Miss Dingley and the test.

11

"YOU'VE GOT to go back to her, Mishmash," Pete said hollowly. "You've got to go back to Miss Dingley's house and stay there until Miss Patch comes home. That's what you've got to do."

Mishmash looked at him, and scratched himself.

"It's not harder than what I've got to do," said Pete hastily. "I've got to face her too." He grimaced. "I've got to take that test. Nothing's going to change that."

Pete thought of the world not coming to

an end, and how much easier things would have been if it had ended. He put his arms around Mishmash.

"That's life, I guess," he said. "You've got to take tests and things. You've got to live through every moment as it comes."

The words sounded familiar to Pete's ears. He had heard them somewhere before. It came to him all at once. That was exactly what Miss Dingley had meant when she had told everybody about tests!

Pete walked Mishmash over to Miss Dingley's house. The gate was unlocked; no one was home. Pete patted the dog encouragingly as he put him inside the gate and locked it.

Mishmash stood up on his hind feet and placed his paws on the wire mesh. It seemed to Pete as if the dog winked at him. But his own eyes were blinking and he figured he could be mistaken. He went around and filled the hole from the outside of the fence and placed an old board across it. Then he started toward home.

Pete walked slowly, up an alley, through an empty lot, across the old orchard beyond the school street.

The weeds grew high between the trees, and the trees were twisted and stumpy. Green apples and pie cherries. But the apples were usually sour and the cherries no good for eating. Some kids had built a platform in one of the trees and an old rubber tire hung from a rope on another. Pete sat down on the rubber tire and wondered what he could say to Miss Dingley.

"You there!" The voice bounced at him from one of the treetops.

Startled, he looked around.

"I'm up in the tree," said a slightly familiar voice. Harsh like Miss Dingley's. Brusque like Miss Dingley's. Pete walked over and looked up into the tree.

"Well, don't stand there and gawk at me," said Miss Dingley. "Help me down. I'm caught."

Pete made a jump and climbed into the tree. He reached a pair of feet encased in tennis shoes, legs in jeans, an old sweater tucked inside a man's belt, and then Miss Dingley's lined face and gray hair.

"The back of my belt is caught in a branch," she explained twisting about.

He worked himself around until he was behind and below her, gave the belt a tug, and it was free.

"Now climb back down," she ordered, "and don't shake the branches. You've got him half frightened to death already."

"Who?" said Pete.

"My owl," said Miss Dingley. "My baby owl. I've been keeping watch for days now, and the mother owl isn't coming back. She won't, you know," she added, "if she's frightened or she thinks someone has disturbed her nest."

Pete dropped to the ground from the lowest branch and stood aside for Miss Dingley to come down out of the tree. She stood on the ground and held the small thing cupped in her hands, but she was looking closely at Pete.

"Oh it's you," she said.

Pete stuck his hands into his jeans pockets.

"Stand back!" she commanded.

Hastily Pete stepped back. Miss Dingley set the owl on a tree stump where it turned its head around and looked the other way.

Miss Dingley bent and examined it closely. "It's starved," she announced straightening up. "It's just plain starved." She went down on one knee and picking up a forked stick began to dig industriously at the soft earth next to the tree trunk. She turned up a small cluster of worms and scooped them up with her hands. She placed a worm on the tree stump next to the baby owl. The owl blinked and swiveled its head again.

"Oh dear," Miss Dingley said, and looked around at Pete.

He stepped back another step. "I wasn't doing anything," he said.

She didn't hear him. She stared off over his head, her forehead creased. She was thinking. After a moment, she nodded. "That's what I'll have to do," she said.

"What?" said Pete.

"A mother owl usually feeds its baby on the fly," she explained, walking several feet beyond Pete. He turned to watch her.

"Watch out," she said, and with small running steps she swooped past the owl, thrusting a worm out at it, as she came abreast of it. The owl turned its head around again and blinked.

"I'm getting its attention," she said with satisfaction. And she darted past the bird again, with a worm. The owl pecked, grabbed the worm in its beak, and gulped.

Breathlessly, Miss Dingley came to a stop a few yards away. "It works!" she said. And made another swoop past the bird.

Pete watched in amazement. "You mean that owl thinks you're its mother?" he asked.

Miss Dingley smiled, a proud thin smile. "I'm very good with birds," she admitted modestly.

Pete felt the grin spreading over his face, felt it widen in all directions—and explode. He doubled up with the ecstasy of it, and then quickly smoothed his face, and straightened his body.

Miss Dingley regarded him balefully.

"I didn't steal Mishmash," he said quickly. "He just ran away by himself."

But the disapproval didn't leave Miss Dingley's face. "Haven't you something more to say to me?" she said sternly.

Pete thought of Leonard McCurdy putting the bubbles in the aquarium. He thought of himself telling the teacher it was Leonard McCurdy. He shook his head.

"No," he said.

Miss Dingley's wrinkles hardened on her face. She gazed at him, with her mouth held tightly closed and her lips stretched back.

"No, what?" she said with a frown.

"No, thank you," said Pete automatically, and turning he marched resolutely away, toward home.

12

WALKING to school the next morning, worry filled Pete. He hurried to get there before Leonard McCurdy and John Williams. If they got to school first, and glued the teacher's desk drawer shut, she would be sure to think Pete did it. The day would be a repetition of the Friday before. Pete shivered.

He elbowed his way through the line at the entrance to the school building and took up a position just outside the door. When the bell rang, he walked as fast as he could without running, for running was forbidden in the school halls, to reach the door to Miss

Dingley's room first. Leonard McCurdy was right beside him. The two boys pushed at each other to take the first place in line before the room door. When the bell rang, Pete dashed in—and stopped short.

Miss Dingley was standing in the back of the room, with a bunch of papers in her hand. The desk drawer was wide open.

Pete smiled triumphantly at Leonard and went to his seat. He took a quick look around. Leonard had also taken his seat. His long legs hung into the aisle. John Williams' feet were stuck out in imitation of his friend. Pete carefully pulled his knees in, and placed his feet squarely under the desk.

When Wanda came into the room, she turned her nose up at Leonard McCurdy and walked straight to her desk. Pete pretended not to see her. He gazed toward the front of the room where Miss Dingley now stood, and his eyes rested on the substitute teacher. She ruffled the test papers in her hands. Regretfully, he wished he had left her sitting up in the tree.

Miss Dingley rapped on the desk. "I will pass out the test questions," she said. "You may start to put down the answers as soon as you receive your copy of the test. We will maintain complete silence," she warned, as she started up the first row. She laid down a sheet of paper on each desk as she moved.

Pete watched the teacher's progress steadfastly. As she drew nearer to him, his stomach lurched. It was like watching the minutes until the world would come to an end, he thought, watching as each sheet was laid on each desk. Pete looked at the paper Miss Dingley put down before him. It was only a little white rectangle with ten questions on it. Only a bunch of yes and no questions. It wasn't the end of the world! Pete laughed out loud.

Miss Dingley turned abruptly. "Who did that!" she demanded.

Gingerly Pete raised his hand.

She looked at him a moment, and a puzzled expression came over her face. "Well, don't do it again," she said, and went on with the passing out of the test questions.

Pete bent his head to the paper. The test was simple, he saw, and he took a deep breath and started in.

Miss Dingley walked up and down between the rows, looking over shoulders. She stopped just behind Pete; she stopped a long time, and he bent over his paper and covered the column of yes and no answers with his left hand.

Pete felt her pencil tap his shoulder. He jerked up his head. "Check your answers," she said.

Pete nodded, but suddenly his heart was beating too loudly. Doggedly he made himself read the last questions. He put down the last answers.

He waited until several of his classmates had risen and laid their completed papers on the teacher's desk, before he arose, and went up to the front of the room. He placed his examination paper on top of the others. Miss Dingley looked at it quickly, and pointed with a blunt finger to the answer on his first question.

Pete blinked. He read the question again, and his answer. It was the wrong answer. Miss Dingley was only trying to help him when she had told him to check his answers again. He looked at her in surprise. Her face looked like a cracked pitcher when she smiled. But he guessed she couldn't help that.

"I made a mistake," he admitted, and shuffled his feet in embarrassment.

"We all make mistakes sometimes," she assured him with a meaningful nod. "The owl is just fine," she added. "Mishmash just loves him."

Thoughtfully Pete regarded Miss Dingley, but she wasn't looking at him. She was gazing out into the room, frowning at Leonard McCurdy whose big feet scraped noisily on the floor under his desk.

"Leonard McCurdy!"

All eyes turned.

"If you have finished your examination paper, will you please rise and bring it to me?"

Leonard grinned weakly. "I can't," he said. "I'm stuck."

The teacher looked surprised. "You're stuck on the questions?"

Leonard shook his head. "No. I'm stuck on my seat."

Wanda Sparling put her hand up to her mouth and the giggle flew out between her fingers. Everyone laughed. But they weren't laughing at the teacher, they were laughing at Leonard McCurdy.

The glue, thought Pete. He must have sat on the instant glue and it had stuck him fast to the seat. Pete grinned.

Miss Dingley walked down the aisle and picked up the test paper from Leonard's desk. Thoughtfully she looked down upon him.

"You wouldn't want to tell us, I suppose,

how you happened to get stuck to your seat?'' she suggested.

Leonard flushed. He looked quickly up at the teacher, then over at Pete.

"I guess I made a mistake," he mumbled. He wriggled, but the seat of his trousers clung steadfastly to the seat of his chair.

"We will ask the janitor to come in at recess time and help you out of your predicament," Miss Dingley said calmly, and turning her back on Leonard, came to the front of the room.

She shuffled the papers on her desk and looked at Pete as if there had been no interruption. "Sometimes it takes a test of some sort to tell us exactly what our mistakes are," she said.

Pete looked out into the room. He remembered how he had feared taking the school examination. He smiled at himself.

From her seat, Wanda smiled back. Hastily Pete looked away. In his mind he could hear her voice saying, "I'll never forget it. Never!"

"I know exactly what you mean," Pete said to Miss Dingley. And scowling at Wanda, he went back to his seat.

ABOUT THE AUTHOR
AND ILLUSTRATOR

MOLLY CONE grew up in Tacoma, Washington, and now lives with her husband and three children in Seattle. The Cone family enjoy swimming, skiing, picnicking, and spur-of-the-moment parties and trips. Mrs. Cone has written many books for young readers, including more stories about Pete and his dog: *Mishmash, Mishmash and the Sauerkraut Mystery, Mishmash and Uncle Looey,* and *Mishmash and the Venus Flytrap.* All of these books are in Archway Paperback editions.

LEONARD SHORTALL was born in Seattle, where he attended the University of Washington. He lives in New York City and is a well-known illustrator of many books for young readers.

POCKET BOOKS

ARCHWAY
PAPERBACKS

Other titles you will enjoy

29948 BASIL OF BAKER STREET, by Eve Titus.
Illustrated by Paul Galdone. The Mystery of the
Missing Twins was one of the strangest and most
baffling cases in the famous career of Basil—
Sherlock Holmes of the mouse world. ($1.50)

29927 PERPLEXING PUZZLES AND TANTALIZ-
ING TEASERS, by Martin Gardner. Illustrated
by Laszlo Kubinyi. A fascinating collection of
puzzles and teasers to challenge your wits, tickle
your funny bone, and give you and your friends
hours of entertainment. ($1.25)

29798 RUNAWAY RALPH, by Beverly Cleary. Illustrated by Louis Darling. This sequel to *The
Mouse and the Motorcycle* continues Ralph's
hilarious adventures when he rides off in search
of freedom and excitement. ($1.25)

29934